CONSUME

HELLISH 1

CHARITY PARKERSON

--Warning: This book is intended for readers over the age of 18.

Copyright © 2017 Charity Parkerson
Editor: Hercules Editing and Consultants
Cover Art: Q Designs
ISBN: 978-1-946099-16-7
All rights reserved.

❀ Created with Vellum

INTRODUCTION

Jonathan thinks Cin is too perfect to be real. He's right.

As the top investigative reporter for *Global Daily*, Jonathan travels all over the world. Three weeks in Tortola, covering the story of the disappearance of twelve women, sounds like heaven. After all, the island is one of the most beautiful in the world. He doesn't have many leads. The women only have one thing in common. They all went missing from the same club—Consume. Fifteen minutes into visiting the club, Jonathan sees him, and the world slips away.

Cinaed, better known as Cin, spots Jonathan the moment he walks through the club's door. It's obvious the man is out of place. Cin slips into Jonathan's mind, catching visions he can't shake. He's never wanted a human for anything other than blood and sex, but Jonathan is different. That's why Cin has to keep the man addicted to being in his bed and send him home safely. There's nothing in Tortola for Jonathan except death.

Once Jonathan's three weeks are at an end, it doesn't take long for him to realize something is wrong. His trip has been—at best—a hazy memory of steamy nights, and he never spent a moment researching his story. No matter how deep he digs into the recesses of his brain, there's nothing except the sexy Scot he met at Consume. With a burning need to know everything, and a deep fear he's been drugged to keep him from his investigation, Jonathan cashes in his extensive vacation time before setting out to break this story. This time, he's determined he won't let anything keep him from the truth, even if it means finding out Cin is the man behind everything.

Author note: This is a short introduction into my new M/M vampire series, Hellish. It was first published in the anthology *Vampires of the Caribbean*.

1

*T*hey met in the most cliché of ways—in a bar. In a club named Consume, no less. Jonathan hated to say their eyes had met across a crowded room. Mostly because the lights were cast low and dozens of gyrating bodies separated them, but their eyes had met across a crowded room. As he'd scanned the crowd, hoping he didn't look as bored as he was, a glimmer of something had snagged his attention. It was the man's eyes. They seemed almost iridescent, reminding him of a wolf. The moment passed as quickly as it happened, making Jonathan wonder if he'd seen anything at all. Still, his gaze lingered for longer than he intended. As if the first time he saw him wasn't like the beginning of a thousand stories, the dude was also tall, dark, and handsome. At the thought, Jonathan turned away. Thirty-two was too old to be so ridiculous.

This trip also wasn't about meeting anyone. Three weeks in Tortola sounded like a dream vacation. For some, it was. For the families of twelve different college-age girls who'd mysteriously disappeared in the last two years, it was a nightmare. That was why Jonathan was there. As an investigative reporter for *Global Daily*, he'd broken more major stories than anyone. Without that stat on his side, Jonathan wouldn't be there, because he had nothing to go on but a location. All twelve women except for one had gone missing from this club. He didn't need this story to make his career, but Jonathan wanted it.

Against his will, Jonathan's gaze slid back to where the sexy man had been standing moments earlier. He was gone. Jonathan swallowed the bitter taste of disappointment filling his mouth. Yeah, he didn't need this story, but he craved the success so he could rub it in his boss's face. A boss who also happened to be Jonathan's ex. The sour flavor of life still coated his tongue. He waved for another shot. The tequila appeared and disappeared in a span of thirty seconds.

As he set the empty shot glass on the bar, a large body collided with his. Before Jonathan had time to turn, warm breath caressed the shell of his ear.

"Dance with me."

He knew. Before turning his head and meeting the sexiest light blue eyes he'd ever seen in his life, Jonathan knew it was his stranger from across the room. The gaze that held his was steady. The man's lips were perfect. Hell, even the dude's eyebrows were flawless. In all his days, Jonathan had never seen anyone as goddamn out-of-this-world as the man awaiting Jonathan's answer.

He took note of the hardcore grunge music blaring through the speakers. "To this?" The instant the words left his lips, the music slowed and the lighting dimmed.

The stranger's lips twisted into a smirk. Jonathan's mouth went dry. The man's fingers linked with Jonathan's. He tugged. "Aye. To this."

Jonathan's knees stiffened, keeping him upright at the

sound of the man's sexy as sin Scottish accent. Without his permission, Jonathan's feet moved. He allowed the man to lead him onto the dance floor. Their gazes never wavered from each other, as the dude walked backward through the gyrating bodies. The crowd parted, making room for them on the floor. When the man's arms finally surrounded Jonathan, he was forced to draw a deep breath slowly though his nose to keep from passing out. It was a mistake. The dude smelled like some delicious spice Jonathan had never tried, but he wanted to. God only knew how badly he wanted to open his mouth over the cords of the man's neck and taste him. Jonathan shook his head, trying to dispel the odd thought.

"What's your name?"

"Cinaed."

Jesus. Even his name was hot. It sounded a bit like Kenny, but with a Scottish lilt that Jonathan wanted to taste on his tongue. "Jonathan," Jonathan said, hoping that by talking he would stop himself from doing something stupid —like capturing a complete stranger's mouth just to feel the man's accent vibrating on his tongue.

Cinaed's hand slid down Jonathan's back, finding the curve of Jonathan's ass. "What brings a man like you to a place like this, Jonathan?"

This. Jonathan bit back the answer. Instead, he picked apart Cinaed's question, as he did everyone's words when they spoke. "What do you mean 'a man like me'?"

The pressure of Cinaed's hand increased on Jonathan's ass as the man drew him closer. "Look around, Jonathan. Do you see anyone else like us here?"

Damn, the way the man kept saying Jonathan's name had him ready to do some naughty shit—like forget why he was there in the first place. He didn't bother looking as

Cinaed demanded. Jonathan already knew they were the only two men dancing together. This wasn't their type of club.

"I could ask you the same."

A low chuckle caressed Jonathan's ear. His dick went hard. "I work here. Your turn."

Jonathan's fingers found the soft hairs at Cinaed's nape. His mind went blank. "It's the closest bar to my hotel," Jonathan said, dodging.

"Lucky me." The words brushed Jonathan's neck a split second before Cinaed's lips touched the same spot. Chill bumps rose on his skin. He swore the tiny hairs on the back of his neck stood at attention beneath the man's touch. They didn't know each other. Jonathan didn't care. He didn't want Cinaed to stop. A haze overtook his mind, making every-thing seem surreal. Cinaed's thumb brushed the small of his back—skin on skin. Jonathan's breath caught at the back of his throat at the contact. Music blared around them, but Cinaed turned his head, as if he heard the small gasp for air. Jonathan turned too, because he couldn't stop himself from doing so. Their gazes met. "No one is watching."

Jonathan didn't care if they were. He couldn't breathe. The iridescent glow he'd seen earlier was back. It was a trick of the light, but Jonathan couldn't focus on anything other than Cinaed's eyes. They were so goddamn beautiful. He felt like he was falling into them. Even as the slow song ended and a faster beat began, their bodies didn't separate. They kept time with the music. Jonathan's heart raced. The man smelled like heaven. It was sweet yet woodsy—like walking through a forest filled with honeysuckle. His body was hard all over. Seriously. Cinaed might have been skinny, but Jonathan could feel every cut muscle. As his fingers traced their lines, Jonathan realized he'd been running his hands over the man's body, shamelessly enjoying his sexy frame.

"I'm about to kiss you."

It was so loud, Jonathan shouldn't have heard him, but he did—like Cinaed was inside his head. His mouth watered in anticipation. Cinaed didn't move. Jonathan couldn't take the suspense. Instead of giving the man a chance to change his mind or get away, Jonathan kissed him. Holy shit. The man's mouth was ambrosia. Cinaed held him. Their bodies still tried to keep time with the music as their tongues clashed. Cinaed's kiss was soft yet deep. He made Jonathan crave feeling that sweet suction around his cock. The man was everywhere. His hands massaged Jonathan's ass, moving against him. Cinaed's erection dug into Jonathan's hip. In all his life, Jonathan had never instantly wanted anyone like he craved the man holding him. It was insanity. He was trapped in the moment with no desire for escape.

THE IMAGES FLOATING through Jonathan's mind had Cin harder than he'd ever been in his life. This man loved sucking dick like most people enjoyed chocolate. Coming in his jeans was a real fear. Cin forgot himself. The moment Jonathan walked through the door, Cin tossed aside his reasons for being there. One glimpse inside the man's head had Cin's feet moving in Jonathan's direction without another thought. Jonathan was there for the same reason as Cin. That couldn't be a good thing.

His fangs grew. Cin pulled back before he gave himself away. He snagged Jonathan's hand and headed for the door. Jonathan came willingly and without question. Cin didn't stop until he had the man alone in the dark alleyway between Consume and the long-closed restaurant next door. As he pushed Jonathan against the wall, his senses kicked in. He could see the man in his arms as clearly as if it was noon rather than midnight. Jonathan's lust coated the air, mixing with Cin's. It smelled like the inside of a sweet shop, causing Cin's mouth to water, and making it impossible for him to call his hunger under control. He could hear the man's heart racing.

Fuck it. Cin pushed his way inside Jonathan's mind, confusing the man's senses. He buried his face in the crook of Jonathan's neck and inhaled. Jesus. The man was like fine wine. Cin licked Jonathan's pulse point, savoring the moment. As his fangs pierced the man's skin, Cin lost control. His fingers sought the button of Jonathan's jeans. Blood filled his mouth as Jonathan's erection filled his palm. The sounds coming from the back of the man's throat had Cin ready to come in his pants. Realization struck. He couldn't stop. Licking the wound on Jonathan's neck, Cin quickly sealed the puncture marks before sliding down Jonathan's body, undressing the man just enough so Cin could get inside him.

He kept just enough control of Jonathan's mind so the man wouldn't see his true nature, ruining their moment. While there, he let the man believe he'd suited up. It was impossible for Cin to contract or spread disease, but he could hardly explain that now. There wasn't an ounce of unwillingness in Jonathan's mind. In fact, the graphic images inside Jonathan's head had Cin wondering if he'd make it inside the man before blowing his wad. This man was a freak. He'd bring Cin to his knees if Cin gave him half a chance.

Using his inhuman strength against Jonathan, Cin had

the man's feet off the ground and around his waist in a matter of seconds.

"Don't worry," Cin said, soothing Jonathan as his thick crown swiped Jonathan's asshole. "I won't let you hurt or let anyone see us." It was a struggle, spreading his power so wide while he was this turned on, but he wanted Jonathan too badly to search out a more private spot. As he sank inside of the man in his arms, a groan escaped Jonathan that nearly crippled Cin. He'd been alive for a long fucking time and he honestly couldn't remember wanting anyone more than the man in his arms. "Goddamn, Jonathan. You're so fucking tight. I won't last long. You have to come for me."

"Give me a reason," Jonathan said, challenging Cin while shocking him speechless. No one had ever resisted his mind control before now. He'd thought the man's reactions were all due to Cin's tight hold on Jonathan's mind, but Jonathan was still clinging to partial control. Anyone else would've orgasmed on Cin's command. Jonathan was still waiting for Cin to fuck something other than his mind. This man was no one's toy. Everything slowed. Cin leaned his weight into Jonathan and pumped his hips, sinking deeper. Jonathan held his stare.

"I'd love to see your eyes during the daylight. They so fucking sexy in the dark."

Cin couldn't breathe. Jonathan was completely lucid and right there with him for every second. "Play with yourself," Cin ordered, hoping to distract him.

"Kiss me," Jonathan said, making his own demands.

With one hand braced on the brick wall at Jonathan's back and one hand gripping Jonathan's ass, Cin leaned in and captured the man's mouth. With his hunger for blood assuaged, he still couldn't will his fangs under control. His lust was too much. If Jonathan noticed, he didn't pull away.

Jonathan reached between them and pumped his cock as their tongues clashed. Pressure drew Cin's balls up tight. He couldn't come before Jonathan. His pride wouldn't withstand it. He tried again, pushing his way inside Jonathan's mind. This time, rather than trying to take control, he let the man see all the different ways he intended to fuck him as soon as he had Jonathan alone.

A long and loud moan vibrated around Cin's tongue. Hot cum hit Cin's chest. *Thank fuck.* He nearly cried his relief. After shifting positions once more, Cin pumped faster inside Jonathan, needing the relief the man's tight ass offered. Pressure crawled up his spine and tightened his balls before pushing against his crown. When his orgasm finally hit, Cin was forced to stiffen his knees against it to keep from going down. Jonathan made him weak. Without thought, his sank his fangs deep into Jonathan's vein, dragging the man's blood into his mouth as he filled the man's ass with his cum.

"Cinaed," Jonathan whispered, sounding more turned on than any man had the right to be.

Cin licked Jonathan's neck a final time. "Most people call me Cin," he confessed against the man's throat.

"Cin," Jonathan repeated, sounding like he was in a fog.

Faolan. I have to take care of this.

Och, I've told you not to do the mind meld thing when you're balls deep in ass.

A low laugh rang through Cin's head. *I have to disappear. You know this man is a priority.*

Aye. Get all up in his shit. Well, you're already there, but you know—

Cin shut down Faolan's incessant rambling before he melted Cin's brain. Not to mention, Cin was still having some impure thoughts about the man in his arms. He didn't want to share any part of Jonathan with his boys right now.

"How far is your room? I'm thinking we're not finished here."

The way Jonathan's eyes still appeared out of focus had Cin ready to pat himself on the back. He always left his partner satisfied. It mattered with Jonathan.

"I thought you were working."

Cin shook his head. He'd forgotten his earlier lie. It wasn't like him to lose himself like this. "Don't worry over it. They can survive the rest of the night without me." According to Jonathan's thoughts, he was in town for the next three weeks. It looked like his team would have to survive without him for longer than a night. He didn't intend to let this man out of his sight until he ushered Jonathan onto a flight back to New York.

hree weeks later...

There were close to two hundred emails filling Jonathan's inbox. He skimmed the subject lines, looking for the most important ones first. It wasn't like he didn't have time to kill. His flight back home to New York didn't leave for another two hours, but still. He hated mundane chores—like opening and reading two hundred fucking emails. There were four from Mike Powers, Jonathan's boss. Each one wanted updates on the very expensive trip to Tortola the company had funded. That was the nicest of the lot. The longer the man's emails went unanswered, the uglier they became. Not that Mike was especially civil at any time since Jonathan had dumped him. That wasn't why Jonathan's stomach shook, bringing him as close to seasickness as he'd ever been on dry land. The more he read, the more he remembered. Twelve missing women. Almost every one had left from the same club where Jonathan met Cin. Jonathan had gone there, hunting down leads. From there, the world slipped away from him.

He remembered Cin and their nights together. At least,

he thought he did. Everything felt hazy or like pieces of every day were missing, the way Jonathan imagined people felt after coming out of anesthesia. Cin drove him to the airport in a white Audi R8. Funny, he could remember everything about the car's interior and Cin's kiss before Jonathan climbed from the car. Yet he couldn't remember anything Cin had said to him. Jonathan could only picture the man's lips moving with phantom words. That was wrong. It had only been an hour since the man dropped him off. Every word that passed between them should be fresh in his mind.

Jonathan sat with his laptop perched on his knees while he stared sightlessly at where the corner met the ceiling. His skin felt cold, but his mind didn't accept it—like nothing was real any longer. From the moment he'd stepped onto that dance floor with Cin, everything changed. Had someone slipped something in that last shot of tequila? If so, it had to have been Cin. One incident of being drugged wouldn't account for an entire three weeks of his life disappearing. He felt sick when he tried picturing anything other than Cin's face. It was as if the man's image soothed him. In truth, he should be more unsettled by the man, who'd obviously done his best to keep Jonathan from learning anything during his trip. Every time he pictured Cin, no anger came. A sense of peace settled over him. It was... odd. He had to stay in Tortola. There was something huge going on there. He could feel it in his bones.

After stuffing his laptop back in his carry-on, Jonathan snagged his cell phone and tried to push Cin's image into a box. He couldn't handle wondering what was going on with him right now. He hadn't done anything with Cin he hadn't wanted, but missing chunks of time—that was scary as hell.

Jonathan couldn't think about it. He might lose his shit if he did. Instead, he called Mike.

"Where's my story?" Leave it to the douche not to bother with saying hello. Jonathan was the magazine's meal ticket. Nothing more. He used that knowledge to his advantage.

"I need more time."

A long silence filled the line. Dread ate at Jonathan's gut. He couldn't explain. If there was a God in heaven, he wouldn't have to try.

"No."

Fuck. "I'm not asking for more money, Mike. The rest of this trip is on my dime."

"You're still there?"

Jonathan thanked every deity listening when his voice came out sounding steady. "Yes. I'm close. I just need a little more time. Like I said, it's on me. I'll fund the remainder of the trip and even use my vacation time. That's how close I am to cracking this thing." He held his breath. Jonathan could hear Mike clicking around on his keyboard in the background. He wondered if his nerves would snap before a loud sigh rang through the line.

"You've built up four weeks of vacation. I suggest you make the most of it."

"Thank you, sir." Jesus. He hated calling Mike "sir," but the man was still his boss. Mike hung up on him. It was just as well. Jonathan had shit to do. He had a nice-sized savings account built up, but it would take every cent for this, and he wanted to get out of this airport as quickly as possible.

"THREE WEEKS."

Cin tied his boots while avoiding Niall's knowing gaze. "Aye. I know."

"Three weeks," Niall repeated. "Knowing we're in the middle of an investigation."

Cin stood and finally met Niall's golden gaze. "If you've got something to say, say it."

Niall shook his head. "I'm old enough to know nothing I say will change anyone's mind about anything other than how they feel about me. Plus, it's not like you don't know how this will end—badly. You should take mercy on that boy and kill him now, before it gets to that point." Without another word, Niall grabbed a bottle of whiskey and headed out the back door. Cin's knee jerk reaction was to chase Niall down and slice his throat, but the man would heal. Their friendship might not survive it. Not to mention, he didn't have time to clean up blood. He needed to make up for the three weeks he'd spent in Jonathan's bed.

The muscles in Cin's stomach tightened at the thought. He already missed the sexy male. That choppy brown hair. His sexy green eyes. Fuck. At six-six, Cin towered over most humans, but at five-nine, Jonathan made Cin feel huge. The man was also slight of build, making Cin wonder if he'd accidentally break him. Those attributes might've made any other man sound weak, but not Jonathan. He was brave and kinky as hell.

A smirk pulled at the corners of Cin's mouth as he drove to Consume. There was nothing he'd suggested that Jonathan turned down. Most men would've cried uncle after the first night. Not Jonathan. Cin had kept the man fed and Jonathan had kept Cin hard. Holy hell. He wanted to jump a plane to New York right now. Maybe, once they had this case wrapped up, Cin would do just that.

GOING to the bar during the day proved to be the thing Jonathan should've done all along. The man working the door had the same story as the police detective in charge of the case. Each woman had left on her own—on foot, as if staying somewhere within walking distance. Jonathan followed the same pathway. The night he'd been to Consume, the path had been low lit but busy. Lots of people walked from hotel to club and back again. Yet there'd been no witnesses who'd seen any of the women from the moment they stepped outside the bar. In fact, surveillance footage from the club's entryway showed the pathway empty.

Jonathan slowly walked the trail. There was a long stretch that had a great view of the water before reaching a place where the path split into several directions, leading to different hotels. Since—for the most part— the women had been scattered throughout, staying at different places, Jonathan worked the theory that whatever happened to them, happened on this long stretch. His eyes strayed to the water. There was a smaller trail, next to a bridge, and leading down to the water's edge. Maybe they were lured from the pathway to the water, or they'd gone willingly, having decided they weren't quite ready to call it a night. An image of Cin, leading him from the club and searching for a private spot to fuck him, hit Jonathan. What if these women had made plans to hook up in the privacy of the jungle surrounding the beach? They could've met someone in the bar, but left separately.

After moving from the bridge's wooden railing, Jonathan stared down the path. There were plenty of places to hide before reaching the beach. They could've dipped between the trees at any time. From there, anything could've happened. Raped, murdered, and dragged to the water. To what means? A waiting boat, maybe? Taken out to sea and fed to the sharks? That would explain the total lack of evidence. His gaze moved to the beach. Was there a place for a boat here? A long pier caught Jonathan's eye. There was a van parked at the opening of the pier and two houseboats tied to the dock. Men milled from van to boat. There were two women, walking like zombies, following in the men's footsteps, as if led by an invisible tether.

Jonathan pulled his phone from his back pocket and started recording. Most likely, it was nothing, but this gave him an idea. What if it was as simple as this? Men snatching women for the sex trade—lured from the club, down to the pier. Once they were shoved onto a boat, they could be anywhere in the world. Living a nightmare and never to be seen again. How sad.

———

THE INSTANT JONATHAN set foot back inside Consume, Cin felt him. He hadn't reached the bar yet, but he could feel Jonathan there, searching for answers. Cin couldn't drive fast enough to get there. His rage knew no bounds. Thank fuck for the overcast sky, allowing Cin to bundle up and step outside without burning alive. Unfortunately, it also meant he was weak, which hadn't mattered when his only plan had been to check out Consume during daylight hours. Now, his powers extended only far enough to help him find Jonathan. The man's location did nothing to soothe Cin's fury. For fuck's sake, he'd sent the man on his way and comforted himself that Jonathan was safely tucked away in New York. Clear of this danger. Now, here the man stood, recording some shit on his phone that was about to get him killed. Dude needed a keeper, for real.

Cin rolled his shoulders, popping his neck. "What are you doing here, Jonathan?"

Jonathan's shoulders visibly stiffened, but he didn't turn. "My job."

"I sent you home," Cin argued, moving closer.

As if his claim raised Jonathan's hackles, the man slowly turned. Crossing his arms over his chest, Jonathan kept his phone pointed toward the dock, still rolling.

"Did you drug me?"

One of the men spotted them. He moved closer—no doubt trying to decide if he should kill them.

Cin had never panicked at the thought of a fight. There'd never been someone like Jonathan for him to consider either. He couldn't let his man get hurt. *His man.* Yes, Jonathan was his, and the dude was a reckless idiot.

"Kiss me."

"Are you fucking insane?" Jonathan asked, his voice rising with every word. "Three weeks of my life are gone. I barely remember you beyond the way you made me feel. Now you want me to kiss you."

"You shouldn't be able to remember me at all," Cin said without thinking. Their party was moments away from getting crashed and Cin needed to get Jonathan the fuck out of there before he got himself killed.

Jonathan's expression turned thunderous. "So you did drug me."

It took every ounce of Cin's willpower not to glance toward the water. Looking like a quarreling couple, rather than someone getting nosy, might be the only thing saving their lives. Cin took a step in Jonathan's direction. Jonathan stepped back. The man heading their way froze, as if realizing they might be completely unaware of him and his activities. Without giving Jonathan time to guess at his intentions, he sprang forward, wrapping the man in his embrace and capturing his lips. Jonathan tried biting him. Like that, crippling hunger rose in Cin's gut. This man was fucking amazing—possibly the bravest human Cin had ever met.

He whispered against Jonathan's lips, bringing the man in check. "Cut it out, baby. You're about to get us killed." Jonathan went still in his arms. Taking advantage, Cin kissed the man for real, stealing what he could before drawing him away from the bridge. He could feel their company, attempting to skim their minds. Cin masked their thoughts, pushing out blatantly sexual images until they reached Cin's car. He opened the passenger side door. Jonathan refused to budge. He eyed the inside of the car before staring Cin down with defiant eyes.

"I'm not going anywhere with you until you tell me what the fuck is going on."

"If you stay here, you're dead."

The man's chin took on a stubborn tilt. "Or I'll have my story."

Cin's temper snapped. He crowded Jonathan's body, forcing him against the open doorway and leaving him two choices—let Cin go flush against his skin or get in the goddamn car. Jonathan stood his ground. Their bodies touched, and—for the first time ever—Cin worried he'd be the one who backed down. "You're interfering with an official investigation. *My* investigation. You have till the count of five to get your sexy ass in the goddamn car or I *will* make you."

Jonathan's features shifted. Curiosity etched his every line. "I spoke with the detective in charge of the disappear-

ance of the women in this area this morning. It
wasn't you."

"I never said what I was investigating. Only that you
were interfering. Get in the car, Jonathan. One. Two."

"Who do you work for?"

"Three."

"If you're in law enforcement, why did you drug me?
That's illegal for everyone, I'm sure."

"Four."

"Unless you're some form of anti-terrorism team. They
usually have hazier rules."

"Five," Cin said, reaching his limit. His mouth collided
with Jonathan's hard enough he tasted blood. His fangs grew
in response. He didn't care nor did he try hiding them as he
deepened their kiss. Jonathan's lust was almost tangible.
Thick enough Cin could taste it. By the time he pulled away,
Jonathan's gaze was unfocused. His vision cleared and Cin
knew. The man remembered—everything. Not just the past
three weeks but the past six years.

"Get in the car." His demand took on a slight lisp with
his fangs at full glory. Jonathan's gaze dropped to Cin's
mouth. Cin didn't try hiding his true nature. Judging by
Jonathan's shock, he was seeing it all. His hardened features.
The slight glow to Cin's irises. The fucking lust dripping
from his pores, because Cin had never coveted anyone or
anything like he did this reckless man who stood against
him now.

"We had a fucking deal, Jonathan," Cin added, because
he couldn't stop. "You get the stories. I get to have your body
and know you're safe. We had a *fucking deal*," he repeated
because his temper was headed south by the second.

Cin wasn't sure if Jonathan gave in or the man's knees
gave out. Either way, he sat. Cin closed the door behind him

before circling the car and slipping behind the wheel. They were nowhere near finished with this conversation, but they needed to have it elsewhere. He seethed as he tried ripping the gears out of his Audi R8 while taking the corners too sharp.

Jonathan didn't make a sound. Of course, it was always this way for the first few minutes of him getting his memories back. Six years ago, he'd met Jonathan in Kirkcaldy while they'd both been handling their version of an investigation. Seven people had been massacred inside a church. Not just killed, but ripped to shreds. Jonathan had been looking for a story. Cin—werewolves. As part of the Hellish Clan, it was his team's job—along with many others—to deal with supernatural crime, punishing the beings involved while reshaping the story in human minds. At the time, he'd seen Jonathan as a means to an end. His position at *Global Daily* was perfect for helping them spread the story they wanted the world to have. Cin hadn't meant to fall in love with Jonathan, but he had—hard.

"Why do you keep refreshing the memory of Mike, making it seem as if we broke up weeks ago instead of years?"

A low chuckle escaped Cin. Jonathan always knew just what to say to cool his temper. "I don't want you to forget to hate that little rat bastard. You're mine." He cast a quick glance Jonathan's way as he made the claim. Cin wanted Jonathan to recognize how serious he was. He'd kill that fucker, Mike, if he ever tried touching his man. Cin downshifted, deciding he needed to slow down. It wasn't Jonathan's fault he was becoming more and more resistant to Cin's memory scrub. Every time, Jonathan seemed to hold on to a little more control.

"Pull over."

Cin glanced over again. Jonathan's hands were balled into fists in his lap and his eyes were locked on the road. "We're almost there."

"I don't give a good goddamn. Pull the fuck over, now."

He tried to read Jonathan's mind. It was a complete black spot. Shit. That couldn't be good. Cin pulled over. The moment the car came to a stop, Jonathan shot from the car and started walking back toward town. Cin jumped out behind him. "What are you doing?"

"Going to get my story so I can go home."

"Fuck, Jonathan," Cin cursed as he raced forward and snagged the man's arm, pulling him to a stop. "I was being serious earlier. You have no idea what you're up against. I can't let you get hurt." Against his will, Cin's jaw hardened as he added, "Nor can I let you print the real story."

Jonathan spun. His eyes. Goddamn. Cin's feet froze to the ground. What he saw in Jonathan's eyes—it looked a lot like hate. "Why do you care if I get hurt? If I'm dead, then you can get off this ride. You can move on with your life. If I'm dead, I can stop losing pieces of me to someone who doesn't really want me."

There was an invisible weight sitting on Cin's chest, suffocating him. "I want you." Even to Cin's ears, his voice sounded tight.

Jonathan took a step forward, making Cin wonder if the man would throw a punch. Instead, he went nose to nose with Cin. "No. You don't. I'm nothing more than a plaything to you. I fucking begged you not to send me away this time. Begged," Jonathan repeated. "Set my pride aside, willing to give up everything, just to be with you. You *do not* want me. Did you even think about what would happen when I got home and didn't have a story—when the people I work with wanted what I'm being paid to do? Did you consider they might think I'm crazy or I would think I'm going insane? Or even worse, did you intentionally leave in bits and pieces of you, so I'd wonder if I'd been slipped a date rape drug or something? Tell me again how you care, Cin. I fucking dare you."

"I don't even know what I'm doing any longer when it comes to you," Cin heard himself admit. "I panic when you're involved. Your safety is all that matters."

Jonathan snorted and walked away again, obviously intent on getting as far away from Cin as possible.

"Jonathan." Cin said the man's name softly, putting his heart into it. Jonathan froze but didn't turn. "I love you." Jonathan's shoulders fell. "I know you love me too." Jonathan tilted his head back and stared at the sky, as if seeking help from a higher power, but he still didn't turn. "Come back with me. See the boys and let us fill you in. If you still want to go, then I don't know."

"At least you didn't lie and say you'd let me go," Jonathan said over his shoulder. He took another step away, as if he still intended to leave Cin behind.

"Faolan is wearing your boots," Cin said, playing his last card and shamelessly throwing his friend under the bus. Jonathan hated that Faolan stole his things when they were apart. Damn. It seemed as if they were apart more than they were together.

Jonathan headed for the car without looking Cin's way. It was obvious he wasn't giving an inch. Still, Cin breathed an inner sigh of relief. He could deal with anything as long as Jonathan didn't leave him.

Load up. We're five minutes out and Jonathan's found something.

Aye, we're on it.

Cin knew there was no need to specify. His team would

be ready to go the second he arrived. Fuck. It seemed things were either all or nothing in his life. He needed to chase down this lead. At the same time, if he left, Jonathan might be out the door right behind him.

Faolan, I need you to stay behind with Jonathan. He's a runner today.

Sure thing.

Now all he had to do was survive a fight with some demons long enough for Jonathan to kill him later.

3

*E*nraged wasn't a strong enough word for the storm of Jonathan's emotions. In fact, he no longer knew why he was so goddamn pissed off, but he was. He was the one who kept letting Cin do this to him. There was nothing stopping Jonathan from walking away right now, going back to New York with his memories intact, and never seeing Cin again. Yep, there was nothing stopping him at all, except everything inside Jonathan. He loved Cin—loved his clan.

The moment Cin had kissed him, six years came rushing back all at once. They were together more often than not, thanks to *Global Daily*. Jonathan always seemed to find his way to wherever Cin had his next big investigation going on. It was as if they were linked in some invisible way. When they'd met in Kirkcaldy, Mike had been more than happy to fund a month of Jonathan's trip. They just broken up, and with Jonathan safely tucked away in Scotland, no one blinked an eye when Mike moved his new man in—the one he'd been sleeping with behind Jonathan's back for almost a year.

Little did Mike know, Jonathan was fine. He'd gone to

Scotland and met the love his life. It just fucking figured when that day came, he'd fallen in love with a vampire. That had come as a bit of a shock. Not that it mattered, since every time Cin left for another investigation, Jonathan was always the first thing the man washed away as if Jonathan meant nothing at all.

A large brick house came into view. It looked exactly like something out of a gothic novel. Vampires did seem to have a sick sense of humor. Cin pulled into the four-car garage and parked. He didn't say anything or look Jonathan's way. For real, the man was pissed off. Jonathan could feel the rage pulsing from his body. Cin jumped from the car before circling around and opening Jonathan's door. One good thing about dating someone over six hundred years old—the dude had awesome manners.

Jonathan moved toward the house. Cin blocked his way, leaving Jonathan no other choice but to meet his stare. The light blue eyes he loved glowed with fury as they focused on Jonathan. It seemed the man had been stewing and reverted to being the alpha on the drive. No trace of his earlier contriteness made an appearance.

"When I tell you to get in the car, like I did back there, you do it. You don't know what you're up against here, and yet you still did what you pleased. If you ever disobey me like that again—when your life is on the line—I will turn you over my knee and tan your arse."

Jonathan's knees weakened. He'd love that.

Cin visibly sucked in a deep breath. "Stop that."

"What?" Jonathan asked, trying to keep his tone innocent.

"You know what, you delicious freak."

Jonathan hid his smile as Cin led him inside. He knew how to make Cin be quiet. His grin slipped away the moment they cleared the door. The men were packing and ready to roll. All except for Faolan. The lone ginger in the group sat relaxed on the couch, as if it was a lazy Sunday afternoon. The asshat was indeed wearing Jonathan's boots. He looked up and smiled as Jonathan came through the door.

"Hey! It's that Jon boy."

The man was so full of shit, but at least he was smiling. Dougal, or the blond beauty of the bunch—as Jonathan had come to know him—was eyeing Jonathan as if expecting him to explode at any moment. He wasn't wrong. Jonathan might lose his shit. Niall was shifting from foot to foot and looking ready to crawl out of his skin. That wasn't new. The man was darker than the rest—like he'd seen some horrible shit and hadn't come out the other side. Both Dougal and Niall were loaded down, as if ready to go to war. With every nervous shift from Niall, the light caught the blade strapped to his waist and glimmered. The man also had a gun Velcroed to his leg, but from what Jonathan had heard, Niall preferred his knife. He was vicious. Loved getting up-close and personal.

"We have to go before we lose their trail," Niall said, practically growling each word. Jonathan wasn't surprised Cin was leaving. Cin was always leaving. He knew what Cin did was bigger than him—bigger than them. His heart didn't care. At the moment, everything hurt. He didn't bother glancing Cin's way. Jonathan wouldn't stand in his way. Instead, he headed for the couch, taking up post next to Faolan. He'd wait. After all, Jonathan had no intention of going anywhere.

Come back to me. Jonathan put the thought out there, hoping Cin heard.

Cin focused on him. "I always do."

Jonathan stared at the door for much longer than he liked after Cin left. He might have done so for the rest of the day if not for Faolan.

"Are you all right?" Faolan asked softly, pulling Jonathan's focus his way. His amethyst eyes glowed for a moment before returning to a more humanlike color.

"I'm fine."

Faolan shook his head. "No. You're not."

A growl rose in Jonathan's throat. "Stay out of my head."

The low chuckle escaping Faolan had Jonathan wanting to put his fist in the center of the man's face. "I'm not in your head. Just digging for info you willingly handed over."

"You're wearing my goddamn boots," Jonathan said, changing the subject in hopes of clinging to his sanity.

The man's contagious smile made it hard for Jonathan to put any real heat behind his accusation. "You're part of the Hellish Clan now." His gaze slipped down Jonathan's body, and his voice turned seductive. "We share everything."

Jonathan drew a slow breath through his nose and kept his mind carefully blank. Fucking vampires. They knew how to drip sex and make anyone want it. Hell would freeze before Jonathan gave any of them the satisfaction. He chose a different track instead. "Obviously, I'm not part of the clan if you keep sending me away."

Faolan grabbed his chest in mock hurt. "I never did any such thing. If it was up to me, you'd never go anywhere. You're quite the hoot when you're nae being all stingy with your shoes and such."

Before Jonathan could respond, Cin came back through the door. "We missed them. Niall stayed behind to keep watch. It's obvious they've been using that port for a while."

"Your man is quite the catch," Dougal said, coming in

behind Cin. "If he hadn't shown up, we'd still be spinning our wheels."

Jonathan flashed the man a grateful smile. No doubt it would be the only credit he got. "What about the women?"

Cin shook his head. "Baby, those women are long dead. Demons aren't known for keeping their victims. They use their bodies for pleasure and what blood they can get to appease their masters. The rest probably went to the sharks."

Jonathan waved away Cin's words. "Not the missing women. There were two women with them, following them from the van to the boat. It was a bit odd, actually. They followed them step by step, almost as if tied by an invisible tether. Look," he said, pulling out his cell phone and cueing up the video he'd captured earlier. They huddled around Jonathan's phone, watching the scene play out. As Jonathan stared down at the device in his hands, his confusion grew. There were no women. "I don't understand. They were there." He pointed out the two men who the women had been following.

At his claim, all three of the men focused on him at once. Jonathan's hand shot to his head as a sharp pain pierced his skull. He tried slamming down a wall. As quickly as it began, the pain stopped.

Dougal shook his head. "Damn, Cin. Your fella is a Traveler. No wonder you can't keep a glamour on him."

Jonathan rolled his eyes. "That's the dumbest thing I've ever heard," he said, still rubbing his forehead. "What does my time spent traveling have to do with anything? And stay the fuck out of my head." All the men continued eyeing him in awe and open interest, as if seeing him for the first time.

Dougal shook his head. "Not a world traveler. A Traveler with a capital T."

Jonathan dropped his hand. "I'm not hearing a difference."

"You can see things," Faolan said, as if it should've been obvious. "Like those women's ghosts following their killers on the dock, which happens quite often, by the way, especially with women. They're strong willed and refuse to leave their murderers until someone avenges them. Anyhow, this means I'm right and you were wrong. Ha! You *are* part of the clan." Jonathan might have been drawn into Faolan's foolishness if not for the way Cin was staring at him. "I hope you know this means I get to keep the boots," Faolan added, as if anyone was still listening.

Cin shoved Jonathan's phone into Faolan's hands. "Here. Look after this." Without waiting to ensure the man complied, Cin snagged Jonathan's elbow and led him away. "We have some things to discuss."

Jonathan let Cin lead him up a flight of stairs and into a large bedroom. It smelled like Cin. Longing washed over Jonathan. Maybe Cin was right to steal the memory of him. This horrible deep pit of need would've been haunting him every second they were apart if Cin didn't take it from him. Cin's fingers skimmed Jonathan's spine. His eyes fell closed at the contact. Who was he kidding? Each time he lost his recollections of their time together, a little piece of him died. He was one of those stupid men everyone talked about. Too weak to walk away from someone who destroyed him.

"Jonathan."

Goddamn it. The way Cin said his name—no doubt the man read his every thought.

"If you're about to say anything to me about returning to New York, then save it. I'm telling you now, if you wipe my memories one more time, you'd better make that shit permanent, because I don't want to ever see your face again." Jonathan didn't turn as he made the threat. He couldn't look at Cin and say those words without breaking, but he meant them. The confusion he'd experienced inside the airport had been the final straw. No one could say they loved him and make him feel that way.

"Look at me."

He wanted to tell Cin to fuck off, but his feet moved without his brain's permission. Jonathan turned. Cin's expression caused the air to seize in his lungs. Cin slipped to his knees and pressed his face to Jonathan's stomach. Jonathan's anger fell away as he wrapped his arms around Cin's head and held him there.

"Sometimes you believe I love you. Other times, you don't feel it at all."

Pain stabbed Jonathan through the chest at Cin's claim. "That's not true." Even Jonathan heard the lie in his voice.

Cin ignored his claim. "Which is it today, Jonathan? Do you love me?"

His chest tightened at the vulnerability in Cin's voice. "So fucking much," Jonathan admitted without shame. Cin's eyes fell closed at his answer, as if relief washed over him. It was moments like these that kept Jonathan from walking away. This man was badass. In fact, he wasn't a man at all. Cin was a deadly beast, but here he was at Jonathan's feet, surrendering himself. After Cin, no one else would ever be enough.

WHILE HOLDING JONATHAN'S GAZE, Cin loosened the button on Jonathan's jeans. Goddamn. If Cin hadn't already been on his knees, the images that fired to life in Jonathan's head would've taken him down. Every time they touched, this man had Cin thanking the gods for bringing them together. Cin was more than happy to bring Jonathan's fantasies to life. He set Jonathan's erection free. Jonathan's eyes lost focus. Cin bit back a smile. Hoping to drag out the man's anticipation, Cin leaned in slowly before licking Jonathan's crown. A moan slipped past his lips as Jonathan's pre-cum coated Cin's taste buds. Nothing tasted better than his man turned on. He'd plan to take his time and make Jonathan beg. It turned out he was the one who couldn't withstand the torment. Jonathan's dick beat at the back of Cin's throat before he realized it would happen. The man's pulse sounded ridiculously loud to Cin's overloaded senses. He could smell the blood pulsing through Jonathan's veins. Cin didn't want to drink anything other than Jonathan's cum. His erection hated him for ignoring it. In nearly seven hundred years, Cin had learned some patience. They'd have time for play later. Right now, nothing mattered as much as stealing Jonathan's orgasm.

Jonathan's muscles tensed. His heartbeat sounded louder than before. The scent of the man's lust over-whelmed Cin, smelling like freaking heaven. When Jonathan's orgasm finally hit, Cin felt more powerful than he had in years—like he could conquer the world. When Jonathan had begun walking down that road, intent on leaving him, Cin had glimpsed a horrible future, one devoid of Jonathan. He would never let that happen. At this moment, with the man's juices filling Cin's mouth, he knew he could make everything right. Jonathan hadn't given up on them yet. He didn't stop swirling his tongue around Jonathan's cock until he'd licked the man clean. The way Jonathan's fingers massaged Cin's scalp had Cin ready to sweep the man into bed and hold him for the rest of the night.

The van is back. There's something strange happening here.

Cin bit back an irritated sigh at Niall's call for assistance. *We're on our way.* Cin came to his feet and captured Jonathan's mouth. As much as he hated it, he had to keep their kiss short. That was all it took to steal his heart all over again—the way Jonathan always did with every touch.

"I'm sorry, baby. I have to go. Niall needs us." He helped straighten Jonathan's clothes.

"It's okay. Go do what you need to," Jonathan said, even as he came in for another kiss.

Shit, guys. Seriously. Need you now.

Cin pulled away. "Goddamn it. Niall's in trouble."

Jonathan pushed him away. "Go."

With a final glance over his shoulder, Cin did as told. After throwing open the bedroom door, Cin readjusted his clothes to ease the pressure on his dick and tried clearing his mind. It was hard with the image of Jonathan's hurt expression still at the forefront of his brain. Cin had wiped the sadness from Jonathan's eyes, but fuck. He hadn't even unstrapped his guns before blowing his man. What kind of lover did something like that? Why did Jonathan want this life? Niall was right. Cin would get the man killed. Jonathan couldn't understand that what they knew from over six hundred years of living, having his memories wiped was the humane thing to do. Life with Cin would be hard and dangerous. There would never come a day when Cin could retire. The only out for him was the final death, which brought with it a whole other list of reasons Jonathan couldn't stay.

No way could Cin watch Jonathan die. That meant, eventually, turning the man. He loved the sexy reporter. There was no one he'd rather be tied to for eternity. But that was just it; Jonathan would be stuck with Cin. No way out.

He wouldn't be a full vampire. Jonathan wouldn't be able to survive on drinking human blood. The only blood that would sustain him was vampire. Jonathan would literally starve to death without Cin or his clan. He didn't know how to start that conversation. Cin loved Jonathan too much to condemn him to that life, but neither could he stay away.

His black mood and dark thoughts kept his brain busy as they traveled to the docks. During the day, he was forced to drive—his powers limited by the sun. The sun had fallen an hour ago, and his senses were at their highest. It was quicker to dissipate and reappear at different points. Each member landed at a separate location, surrounding the pack of demons. Cin put Jonathan out of his head. One demon on his own was dangerous enough. A pack, that was beyond deadly, and intriguing. Demons didn't tend to work together.

We need to take at least one alive. There's something verra odd about this.

Dougal was quick to agree. *For real, I got a bad feeling in my gut.*

The van Jonathan had captured on video sat parked at the end of the dock once more. A houseboat was tied to the wood, making an odd scraping noise with every lapping wave. Cin opened his senses, searching the thick brush for anything unnatural.

Niall.

No answer came to Cin's mental call.

"Found him," Faolan said, startling Cin with his sudden appearance. Cin followed on the giant vamp's heels, ducking between trees until he spotted Niall's still form on the ground. He was unconscious and bleeding but alive.

"What the fuck?"

A snarl was all the warning they got before the beach

came to life. At least seven possessed humans appeared from the trees, falling on them like the beasts that now owned their bodies. There was no sense in sparing them from damage. The men's souls had fled their vessels long ago. Any hint of soul left behind would've broken from the taint of evil. Cin pulled two guns from their holsters in one motion, firing at two demons, protecting Dougal as the other vamp helped Niall.

His arm is shredded. They have hounds somewhere.

With a mental nod, Cin split his attention between Dougal's report and keeping them safe. *Get him up and send him home. I'll make sure we're not followed.*

* * *

SOMETHING WAS WRONG. Jonathan could feel it in his bones. He'd been standing at the sink, intent on filling the coffeepot and settling in for a long night when a horrible sense of foreboding solidified in his chest. Jonathan kept his gaze carefully locked on the water pouring from the faucet. He wanted to reach out for Cin the way all the men spoke to each other. Since he couldn't, Jonathan brought an image of Cin as he'd been earlier to mind. He pictured every detail from the tight-fitting t-shirt to the military-style boots. Jonathan hoped his efforts would bring about some mental connection. Perhaps Jonathan couldn't reach out to Cin, but Cin could hear him. His skin tingled with awareness. Cin was coming. He could feel him. Jonathan was equal parts amazed and terrified. The sense of something horrible looming didn't ease. Even knowing he was coming, Jonathan still startled when a warm weight pressed against his back. His heart sped with fear—not lust. It wasn't Cin.

Jonathan knew without having to look. This man was larger, imposing.

"Close your eyes, gorgeous." Niall's voice caressed Jonathan's ear with each syllable. Jonathan did as the man said. Niall was darker than the rest. He always watched Jonathan with something akin to hatred.

"I don't hate you. Don't open your eyes."

The man's arms encircled him. Water splashed. He could smell the bitter taint of copper. Did the water run red with blood from today's victims? Would this man kill him? Jonathan kept his breathing steady by force of will alone.

"I have no intention of harming you."

"Stay out of my head," Jonathan said out of habit.

Niall's hot breath brushed the shell of Jonathan's ear. "Unlike Cin, I don't have a choice. He can control it. I hear everything. All the time. It's never quiet anywhere I go."

Jonathan's heart squeezed in his chest. That sounded like hell. He loved the quiet.

"You can open your eyes now."

Jonathan's lids lifted. His gaze dropped to the hands boxing him in against the counter. They were red from Niall scrubbing them. Splotches of blood still speckled the inside of the sink. Niall immediately rinsed them away.

"You're too nice for this life," Niall said. His tone sounded conversational, but Jonathan didn't know how to feel. The man was obviously trying to protect him from the ugliness of the day. Yet he didn't move away, making Jonathan wonder over his intentions.

"Where's Cin?"

"Ensuring we weren't followed. You know he'll wipe your memories again, right? He loves you too much to let you stay." Jonathan understood then. He was being held captive for Niall's lecture. "I see everything inside your head and everything inside his. No one can shut me out. If you want to leave here with your memories intact, you'll..." Niall paused. His weight increased against Jonathan's back. As Jonathan looked on, a fresh trail of blood ran down Niall's arm into the sink. He stared at the flow in confusion. Horror sank in. It had been Niall's own blood he'd been washing away.

"Apologizes. Didn't realize I was so weak."

Jonathan spun in Niall's hold. "Holy shit. You're hurt." He went hunting for wounds, but Niall pushed his hands away.

"Nay worry ov'r me," Niall said, his brogue thickening in his weakness.

Jonathan couldn't let this go. Instead of trying to tend to Niall's wounds, Jonathan pulled the neck of his shirt down and turned his head, offering Niall his throat. "Take my blood, then."

"Cin... "

"No one owns me," Jonathan said, sounding more bitter than he intended. "Plus, you're hurt. That takes priority."

"He woul' nay care. You're his."

A loud growl—like nothing Jonathan had ever heard before—rent the air, followed by gunfire. Jonathan jumped. Niall let out a string of curses Jonathan had never heard but knew were bad. Niall moved as if to push away. Jonathan snagged his shirt, stopping him.

"Take my blood first. You're no good to anyone if you keel over." Niall's golden gaze met his. He felt the man's hesitation. "It's not like it's sexual or anything. Just do it," Jonathan said, exposing his neck once more.

Niall shifted closer. His hot breath brushed Jonathan's skin before his mouth opened over Jonathan's pulse. Goosebumps rose on Jonathan's skin. Their bodies collided as

Niall's fangs pierced Jonathan's skin. Jonathan made a terrible discovery. He'd been wrong. It *was* sexual. He'd always believed the way he felt when Cin took his blood was due to their relationship, but he'd never been more wrong about anything in his life. Niall's hard cock dug into Jonathan's hip. Jonathan tried holding still. The temptation to rub against the man like a cat was a real thing. His erection beat a pattern against the inside of his jeans, leaking and begging for relief. He hovered on the edge of orgasm, and if Niall didn't stop soon, Jonathan feared coming in his jeans was a real possibility. Niall licked the puncture marks, sealing them. Jonathan thought he might have whimpered. It was out of his control. Their gazes met. Jonathan wondered if the vampire would kiss him. The back door flew open. Splintering wood flew in every direction. Niall leapt away from Jonathan, pulling his blade from his belt and placing himself between Jonathan and the demons pouring inside.

Without thought, Jonathan went for the butcher's block, and grabbed the largest knife he could find. It never occurred to him he should run. This was his clan. They were in danger. His fear meant nothing in the face of that knowledge. He would fight. A red and yellow set of eyes locked on to him. Images so horrific that Jonathan almost hit his knees raced through his mind. Evil and sulfur coated the air, choking Jonathan. Terrifying screams of the long dead sounded in Jonathan's ears. They were real, but they weren't. It was an echo of past sins, consuming Jonathan. Four vampire warriors stood at his side, and still Jonathan's knees tried buckling under the fear and mental torment. Those poor women never stood a chance. In a blinding moment of clarity, he understood everything—why Cin's job was so much more important than their relationship, and how

Jonathan would soon be dead. He saw his death as clearly as if it had happened already. Perhaps Dougal had been right after all. Jonathan had some form of extra-human ability of sight. As the thought passed through his head, a cool pressure touched his neck a half second before a sharp pain sliced through his throat, tearing away his ability to swallow or breathe. The floor rushed up to meet him. Shouts, growls, and gunfire continued around him. It all sounded as if coming from inside a long tunnel. Nothing felt real. There was a huge disconnect from reality that Jonathan couldn't penetrate. Niall's face appeared above him. The man looked so different than he had only minutes earlier when Jonathan had been so certain Niall was about to kiss him.

"Cin," Niall yelled. "I need you to tell me what to do. Mercy or damnation?"

There was no air. Jonathan cupped his throat, choking. He didn't feel the pain any longer, only the suffocating. The world turned hazy around the edges. Life was slipping away. He wanted Cin. Niall looked freaked. He'd never seen the man anything other than eerily calm. That was how Jonathan knew there was no hope. He was dead.

"Niall, do not let my man die," Cin yelled, sounding winded.

The man hovering over him focused on Jonathan. Everything went calm. There still was no air, but the fear slipped away. Niall's eyes glowed yellow for a moment. "Damnation it is," Niall said in a quiet tone. The man's hand rose to his mouth. His fangs extended, ripping open his wrist. Niall pushed Jonathan's hands away from his slashed throat. Warmth dripped into the wound, reminding him of the pain he'd thought was gone. Niall glanced over his shoulder. "Cin, finish this. You know I cannot."

Cin came into sight. He was covered in sweat and blood.

"Switch," he yelled. In a flash, Niall shot to his feet, taking over the man's fight while Cin dropped to his knees next to Jonathan. His gaze moved over Jonathan. "Och, baby. I never wanted this for you, but I can't let you die. Losing you would destroy me."

He tried opening his mouth and telling Cin he didn't want to die either, but no sound emerged.

Cin shook his head. "Don't try to talk. I need you to do something. You won't like it." Just as Niall had, Cin used his fangs to rip open his wrist. Unlike Niall, Cin pressed his sliced wrist to Jonathan's mouth. "You have to drink my blood, baby. If you don't, you'll die. If you do drink it, you also won't be like me, but you will be trapped with me."

Jonathan didn't hesitate. Hot metallic liquid filled his mouth. He was too out of it to think about anything other than surviving. Not only did Jonathan like living, he wanted to be with Cin forever. He'd known all along that would mean—one day—he'd have to give up his humanity. Jonathan tried swallowing. Nothing happened. The panic in Cin's expression said as much as the darkness crowding Jonathan's vision. Now, not only did everything sound like he was in a tunnel, it looked like it too. He tried focusing on Cin's gorgeous eyes. His vision wouldn't clear. There was no fear or pain, only exhaustion. His lungs burned from lack of oxygen. When the darkness settled over him, carrying him away, all Jonathan felt any longer was relief.

4

———

"*D*o you plan to lounge around forever?"

Jonathan glanced around at the shadows surrounding him. Niall appeared like smoke, taking the shape of a man before solidifying. Jonathan glanced down. He needed to know if he looked the same. Unlike Niall, his body was still solid but didn't feel real—like being trapped in a dream. The last thing he remembered was struggling for air. That didn't seem to be a problem any longer.

"Am I dead?"

Niall's mouth lifted in one corner. "No."

He glanced around again at his slightly less than clear surroundings. Nothing seemed to have a solid form, other than them. "Is this a dream?"

"Do you want it to be?"

Jonathan shook his head, trying to clear away the cobwebs. "I'm not sure."

A full-blown smile exploded across Niall's face. The breath caught at the back of Jonathan's throat. He'd never seen Niall smile. It was mesmerizing. He had dimples. "Aye, well, if you'd like, you can tell yourself this was a dream when you open your eyes and rejoin the living."

"So I am dreaming?" Jonathan asked again, trying to keep up.

Niall sighed. "How about you just listen for a few minutes?"

Jonathan nodded, at a loss as to what else he could do but obey.

Niall crossed his arms over his massive chest and rocked back on his heels, as if trying to decide where to start. Jonathan stood still, expecting anything. A part of him still suspected he might be dead and this was all part of his trip to the afterlife.

"We got interrupted the last time we spoke," Niall said, taking Jonathan by surprise with his choice of topic. "You had questions you didn't get to ask."

"Did I?" So much had happened in such a short period of time, Jonathan couldn't remember. Dying had wiped him clean.

"Aye," Niall said, holding his gaze. "You wanted to know why I thought you should leave us behind, but you were scared to ask."

"I don't know if scared is the right term."

Niall blew out a breath and shook his head at Jonathan's rambling. "I thought you were going to listen."

Jonathan motioned for him to continue. "Sorry. Go on."

"For whatever reason, you didn't want to ask," Niall said, conceding to Jonathan's interruption. "When you open your eyes, you may not see me for a little while, so I wanted to answer your questions before I go."

"Where are you going?"

"Away," Niall answered, obviously not intending to expound. "Don't worry. We have forever and some years will go by in the blink of an eye while others will drag on for what feels like an eternity."

So they'd turned him after all. He wanted to ask, but Niall didn't give him a chance.

"I didn't want this for you. It's not personal. I wouldn't want this for anyone. Our clan is small, and now you're completely dependent upon us for survival for the rest of your days. We were born this way. You were not. Most of the skills we possess won't pass to you, and drinking human blood will not sustain you. You'll need to drink from one of us to live. That's what I didn't say to you before we were interrupted."

"Are you saying you don't want me sucking on your neck the way I let you suck on mine?" Jonathan asked, trying to ease the heaviness coating the air.

Something dark—like deep hunger—passed over Niall's features. "Anytime you need me, you may call to me and I will come to you."

For some reason, one Jonathan couldn't explain, that sounded oddly ominous.

"There are a million tiny details about this life you need to understand. You'll have to learn a whole new way of living. Cin will be with you every step of the way."

"Why isn't he here now?"

"Who says he isn't?" Niall shot back just as quickly, causing Jonathan to have more questions than before.

"Why are you here now?"

Niall moved closer, crowding Jonathan's space. Jonathan let it happen. The man's golden gaze flared to life, glowing bright, as if attempting to dig for info Jonathan didn't want to give. "I told you—I have to go away, and you had another question I didn't get to answer."

"What?" Jonathan had no idea why he was whispering, but there it was.

"You wondered if I would do this," Niall said, swooping in and covering Jonathan's mouth with his. The giant vamp's kiss was a hell of a lot sweeter than Jonathan ever would've imagined. He gently cupped Jonathan's face between his hands, as if savoring the moment. In the back of his mind, Jonathan knew he should shove Niall away. This wasn't fair to Cin. He didn't want anyone other than Cin. Did he? Fuck it. As Niall had said earlier, this was just a dream. Soon he'd open his eyes and realize none of this had been real, or the angel of death would appear, escorting Jonathan to his final resting place. Either way, this moment didn't count. Jonathan kissed Niall back. It wasn't like when he kissed Cin or even when Niall had taken his blood. Their tongues met and stroked. There was a definite lover-like feel to their touch, but it wasn't the sort of passion that burned a person to the ground. This was something else.

Niall was the first to pull away. With his eyes closed, Jonathan held on to the man's shirt, keeping him in place. Not that Niall seemed in any hurry to escape. He kept his forehead pressed to Jonathan's and his breaths came in loud gasps. Jonathan could feel the man's large frame expanding with every deep lungful of air. Every sensation seemed heightened—twice as much as anything he'd ever experienced before.

"Eternity is a damn long time, Jonathan," Niall said softly. "Even if you spend it hating me, I swear I'll come to you when you call." The same as he appeared, Niall disappeared—like smoke seeping away. Jonathan stared at the empty space where he'd been only moments earlier. He didn't have time to puzzle out the experience.

The sensation of light kisses touched his stomach.

Jonathan glanced down at this body. His shirt was gone. Hadn't a gray t-shirt been covering him the last he looked? The pressure of lips skimming his stomach happened again. Jonathan automatically lifted his hand, searching for the source. It landed on something solid. Soft locks of hair slipped across his palm. Jonathan blinked. Light blinded him. He slammed his eyes closed against the assault. The kisses moved up his body. The sensation of floating overcame him.

Jonathan's eyes fluttered open once more. This time, he prepared himself. It wasn't as bright this time. In fact, there was barely any light at all. He was in Cin's bed. Jonathan slipped his fingers through the man's hair once more.

"Cin?" He instantly regretted his attempt as speaking. It felt like he'd swallowed razor blades and sounded like it too.

"Aye, baby. You're finally awake."

"Hurt," he croaked out, hoping Cin wouldn't expect more.

"Don't try talking. You're still healing."

But I have questions. Jonathan couldn't contain his internal pout. He'd expected things to be different. No pain, for one damn thing.

And I have answers, but there's plenty of time.

Jonathan nearly levitated in his happiness. *Oh my God. I heard you. In my head, and you heard me. Holy shit. We spoke.*

A low chuckle caressed Jonathan's chest as Cin kissed a path up his body. "Trust me, baby. The novelty will wear off soon."

I saw Niall. In my dreams. Does that mean it was real?

While straddling Jonathan's hips, Cin sat back on his heels and stared down at him. Something dark passed over his features. "Aye, most likely."

He said he was leaving.

"Aye." Cin looked sad.

Jonathan's chest hurt—like he was missing a part of himself. He couldn't make it stop. He blinked against the sudden onslaught of pain.

Cin slid down, wrapping Jonathan in his hold, as if trying to hold him together for a mental break he knew would soon come. "I'm so so verra sorry," Cin whispered. His brogue thickened. "Something went wrong when I tried saving you. My blood wouldn't heal you. Niall had to be the one. Your bond to him will be stronger than what you feel for me."

The pressure in Jonathan's chest increased by the second —like he could sense Niall moving farther away. *Nothing could ever be stronger than what I feel for you.* Jonathan ran his fingers through Cin's hair, trying to ease the man he loved even as his heart slowly crushed from an invisible weight.

"It's okay. I'd rather have some of you than none."

"Kiss me," Jonathan croaked out, because he couldn't take the pain in Cin's voice any longer. He fucking hated that the man he loved more than he had his life was apologizing for doing what had to be done to save him.

Cin shifted positions until no more than an inch separated their faces. "Eternity is a damn long time."

That's the same thing Niall said. Please kiss me.

"He wasn't exaggerating. I've been alive going on seven hundred years and it took me this long to find you. I love you."

A smile pulled at Jonathan's lips. Some of the tension in his chest eased. "I love you too," Jonathan mouthed because it hurt too much to say it. Instead of asking again, Jonathan pulled Cin's head down and captured the man's lips. The instant their tongues met, a crack formed in his mind, splitting Jonathan in two. He loved this man so goddamn much, yet a roar of denial still sounded in his ears, so loud it almost seemed real. Jonathan wasn't the furious one. It was Niall.

The End.

KEEP an eye for the next book in the Hellish series, Devour myBook.to/DevourHellish

You can find updates on my website www.charityparkerson.com/hellish or you can sign up for my newsletter

ABOUT THE AUTHOR

Charity Parkerson is an award winning and multi-published author with several companies. Born with no filter from her brain to her mouth, she decided to take this odd quirk and insert it in her characters.

*2015 Readers' Favorite Award Winner
   *Winner of 2, 2014 Readers' Favorite Awards
   *2015 Passionate Plume Award Finalist
   *2013 Readers' Favorite Award Winner
   *2013 Reviewers' Choice Award Winner
   *2012 ARRA Finalist for Favorite Paranormal Romance
   *Five-time winner of The Mistress of the Darkpath

Connect with her online:

--Website: charityparkerson.com
   --Facebook: facebook.com/authorCharityParkerson
   facebook.com/TheMenofSin
   --Twitter: twitter.com/CharityParkerso

www.charityparkerson.com

www.ingramcontent.com/pod-product-compliance
Lightning Source LLC
Chambersburg PA
CBHW060356180626
46817CB00008B/3036